Aberdeenshire
COUNCIL

Aberdeenshire Libraries
www.aberdeenshire.gov.uk/libraries
Renewals Hotline 01224 661511

First published in 2014 in Great Britain by
Barrington Stoke Ltd
18 Walker Street, Edinburgh, EH3 7LP

www.barringtonstoke.co.uk

Text © 2014 Mary Hoffman

A CIP catalogue record for this book is available
from the British Library upon request

ISBN: 978-1-78112-402-4

Printed in China by Leo

ANGEL
of
VENICE

MARY HOFFMAN

Barrington Stoke

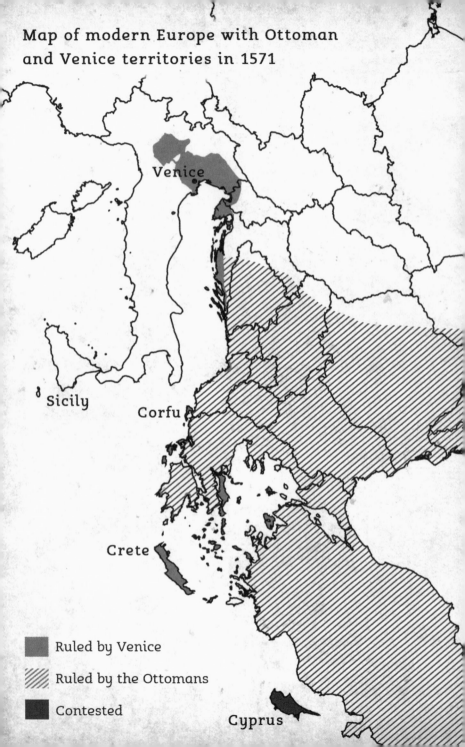

Map of modern Europe with Ottoman and Venice territories in 1571

Venice

Sicily

Corfu

Crete

Cyprus

Ruled by Venice

Ruled by the Ottomans

Contested

CONTENTS

1

A Growing Boy

"Fetch the water, Luca!"

"Chop the wood, Luca!"

"Luca, light the fire!"

All my life, people had been telling me what to do. And what not to do.

"Don't cheek your brother!" they would say.

"Listen to your father!"

"You mustn't steal fruit!"

The last one was very hard to obey. I was a growing boy of 16 and I was always hungry.

There weren't all that many gardens in Venice but there were some near our house with fruit trees whose branches hung over their walls. So wasn't that fair game?

But my parents were very strict. I mustn't take the fruit.

I was the youngest of seven children. My three big brothers worked with our father in the great shipyard of Venice – the Arsenale. They were carpenters, and they worked with all the different kinds of wood that warships are made of. The galleys of Venice were supposed to be the best ships in the world. They were built to last. You could fling an ordinary warship together in a shorter time but the Arsenale was famous for its careful work and the high quality of its galleys.

For the last few years I had worked there too, but I was not trusted with much important work. My main job was sweeping up the wood shavings and putting them in bags to take to the blacksmiths to feed their fires. And there were always a few bags to take home for our family's cooking fire.

But every now and again, Father showed me how to do something more skilled, like planing the walnut wood that was used for the stern of a galley.

I loved the swirling shapes the plane revealed under the surface of the wood. And I loved the smell of the workshop. But all the dust and shavings made me so thirsty. There I was, only feet away from the canals, surrounded by water but always with such a dry throat.

At the end of the day, when I walked home carrying the bags of shavings, the sight of ripe peaches hanging from the trees that leaned over the walls of rich men's houses was just too tempting.

"You'd better wipe your mouth before you go indoors," my friend Fina said, "or your parents will beat you for stealing fruit again."

Fina lived in the building next door. She and I had known each other since we were babies. Her mother was a widow who took in washing, and as we grew up, we often met at the well in the middle of the square where we lived.

There was always a line of people waiting to fetch water from the well so we had plenty of time to talk.

Fina was the first person to find out that I did not want to be a carpenter like all the other men in my family. What I wanted was to go to sea.

"Well I don't want to be a washerwoman," Fina would say, "but what choice do I have?"

"Maybe you will marry a rich man?" I said. "Then you wouldn't have to work. You are pretty so perhaps a count or even a prince will come into the square one day and see you and take you to live in his grand house."

"Well if that ever happens," said Fina, "I promise you can come and eat the peaches and apricots from our garden. No need to steal them."

But she didn't really think that would be her future. And in the end it wasn't a rich young man who came into our square – it was a rich young woman.

Angelina Santo was from one of the oldest noble families in Venice and the minute I saw her, I fell madly in love with her.

"Close your mouth before you catch a fly in it," Fina said, the day we first saw Angelina cross the square with her servant woman.

"Can you see her too?" I asked. "Or am I having a vision? Surely that is an angel?"

"Looks like a girl to me," said Fina. "A girl who has never had to fetch water from a well or wait in a line for anything."

"But what a girl!" I said. "Her hair is as gold as an angel's in a painting. Her skin is like the flesh of a white peach."

"You better had run away to be a sailor," said Fina. "I don't think you'll ever be a poet."

I took no notice of my friend. "But what is she doing in our square?" I asked. "I've never seen her before. I would remember."

"No idea," Fina said. "She looks as if she's on her way somewhere."

It took many months for me to find out that my angel walked twice a week to a lesson with a famous music teacher – he was too disabled to walk to her house. And it took even longer to find out her name. In the end, Fina learned it from a friend.

But soon I learned the angel's routine and I made sure I was always in the square when she passed, if I was not at work. I started to leave the shipyard early on Thursdays so that I could see her walk back from her lesson.

One day I bowed to her.

My reward was to hear her laugh, like the water tinkling in a fountain.

After that, I always bowed when I saw her and she always gave me a smile, even though her servant woman frowned at me.

From then on, I thought of nothing but how I could manage to speak to Angelina. How I could give her a present that would make her notice me.

I was so obsessed with Angelina and her beauty that I didn't really notice what was going on in the shipyard. My father and brothers were working extra hard and I had even more bags of shavings to carry home each day.

If I hadn't been so busy thinking about Angelina, I might have realised why Venice needed more and more galleys made at top speed.

The city was going to war.

2

Rumours of War

Ever since I was a little boy, I had heard stories about the terrifying cruelty of the people called the Ottomans. When I was naughty, my mother threatened me that the Ottomans would come and cut off my ears!

So at first I didn't take much notice of the new rumours that were flying round the city. But I did notice more and more people were carrying swords and daggers.

I didn't know much about politics but I did know that there was more to Venice than just the city I had lived in all my life. There were islands in the Mediterranean Sea with magical names that I longed to sail to – Cyprus, Crete and Corfu. They all belonged to Venice but the Ottomans wanted them for themselves. There had been a big fight over Cyprus last year and now people were saying that the Ottoman fleet had arrived in Corfu.

I didn't even know where Corfu was, but I started to listen to what my father was saying.

"We can't work any faster," he grumbled. "You know we turned out 25 galleys in one month last year? It's mad – it takes 20 men a year to build a good galley."

"Why do they need so many?" I asked.

"Why do you think?" my brother Tommaso asked. "To go to war against the Ottomans!"

"Open your eyes and look around you," my father said. "Have you ever seen the Arsenale so busy?"

It was true. It was always busy at the shipyard but now I could see that there was even more going on than usual. There were a dozen fires where up to a hundred big sweaty blacksmiths were constantly at work and a dozen foundries to make cannon for the ships.

To get to the timber yard, I had to walk past the loft where hundreds of women worked on sails for the galleys. Most days I put my head down and walked as fast as I could because they teased me, calling me their "sweetheart".

But now I came to think of it, the women had been silent for weeks. They were working too hard to spare time to flirt with a teenage boy.

My father was right – I had been walking about with my eyes closed. Or as good as, because all I could see in my mind's eye was the image of Angelina – my Angel of Venice.

Now I began to feel a different sort of excitement. If there really was going to be a war, then perhaps I could somehow be taken on board a galley?

It wasn't how I'd planned to go to sea but it might work.

But then, what about Angelina? I might not ever come back if I went to sea on a war galley.

I talked to Fina about it when I went to fetch water that evening.

"Do you think they'd take me on a galley when they set out to fight the Ottomans?" I asked.

"At last!" she said. "A proper conversation – one that isn't about Angelina Santo!"

I tried not to listen. "Only, if I went away, I couldn't see Angelina any more," I said.

Fina rolled her eyes.

"And if you stay here?" she said. "What will happen then? You will go to Angelina and say, 'I love you – please marry me,' and she'll say, 'Of course – I've always wanted to marry a carpenter's son – you can build me a house.' Don't be such a noodle."

I was hurt. "Don't be mean, Fina. I know I don't have anything to offer her now but maybe I can make my fortune if I go to war. There may be a lot of treasure to plunder on the Ottoman ships."

"There may be," Fina agreed. "But won't there also be lots of fierce Ottomans with guns and daggers?"

I kept silent. I felt confused. I might never get a better chance to escape a future just like my father's and brothers' but Fina was right – it would be very dangerous.

"And what would you do on board a ship?" Fina asked. "You can't be one of the rowers – you aren't strong enough."

She was right. The hundred or so men who pulled the oars on each galley were much older than me. They were often tough and dangerous convicts who had been offered a pardon for their crimes if they took part in a battle.

"You can't be one of the soldiers either," Fina said. "You don't know how to load and fire a gun, do you?"

"But I've seen boys on the ships," I said. "They run to and fro on deck with shot and powder for the guns and cannon."

"That sounds really dangerous," said Fina.

"Well then, I must tell Angelina how I feel before I go," I said.

But I didn't feel as calm as I sounded. Or as brave.

*

It was the start of August and Venice was very hot. The heat from the forges and foundries in the shipyard was too much to bear. Blacksmiths and foundry men came out from their work as often as they could to drink from the pumps and to pour buckets of water over their heads and shoulders.

Their skin was blackened from their work and the muscles in their arms and backs bulged and made me realise just how weak I was compared with these tough men.

I began to worry about how I would cope in a sea battle. And yet I was normal for my age – I was not very tall but I was wiry and able to cope with hard work. It was just that I had no idea what life on board ship would be like.

But I couldn't get my last conversation with Fina out of my mind. Was she right about the dangers? Could I cope with brutal Ottomans hurling themselves on to our galleys, screaming and firing guns and waving sharp swords?

On the way home that evening the peaches looked so juicy and my mouth was so dry that I could no longer resist. And so I gave in. I pulled three ripe peaches off one branch of a tree that spilled over the walls of a rich man's house.

I ate one there and then, to help my dusty throat. But when I reached our square, I saw Angelina walking towards me and for once she was alone!

I didn't give myself time to think. I just offered her the two juicy peaches, without a word.

And maybe she was thirsty too after her music lesson.

Because she took them. She didn't speak to me but she gave me the nicest smile ever.

I danced in the square like a madman when she had gone.

Angelina had smiled at me and taken a present from me!

Fina saw it all but I didn't stop to speak to her. I didn't want her to spoil my first proper meeting with my angel. I rushed home to be on my own and dream.

3

Nico

And that was how I lived my life for the next week. I dreamed of a beautiful girl. And I dreamed of going to war. And I dreamed of ways to fit the two different ideas together.

In my mind I sometimes came home with my arms full of treasure to lay at Angelina's feet. But other times I'd have a vision of returning to Venice with nothing but horrible wounds – missing an arm or leg.

The worst I imagined was that I didn't come back at all – my lifeless body floated in some far-off sea while a battle raged around my corpse.

I was driving my father mad.

"Luca! Stop daydreaming and come and give me a hand over here," he said.

"Sorry, Papa. But is it true that the fleet is setting out soon?"

"Yes, it's true," he said. "That's why there is no time to waste."

"Where is it going?" I asked him. "To Corfu?"

"No," he said. "The fleet is going to Sicily to meet up with the other ships of the Alliance."

My father didn't often say much so I was as helpful as I could be that afternoon. And bit by bit, I got all the information out of him.

The Alliance was Venice, Spain and the Pope. They were all sending galleys and soldiers to fight the Ottomans. But the Ottomans weren't in Sicily. The Alliance would meet there, but the Ottomans were much further east. If our ships didn't get to them by October, it would be too late to go to war because the weather would change.

That was why the shipyard was so busy. Now everyone was under orders to produce fully armed ships in a very short time so that they could sail down to Sicily and join the rest of the fleet.

In the end I must have asked too many questions, because my father's eyes narrowed.

"Why do you want to know all this anyway?" he snapped. "It's not as if you will be going anywhere near the fleet."

"No, Papa," I said. "I'm just interested, that's all."

He grunted and I kept my head down. He had come a bit too close to finding out my plan.

Not that I had a proper plan.

But, whenever I had a break from the workshop, I started hanging around the other end of the shipyard. That was where the finished ships were launched into the water. And that's where my eyes were really opened.

There were all sorts of people down there – big tough men who were going to pull the oars and drive the galleys across the sea and sun-browned sailors who would run the ships.

But the ones I liked to see best were the soldiers – the fighting men who would fire the cannons and the guns. The ones who would fight hand-to-hand with the Ottomans, armed with swords and daggers.

They were all so cheerful and confident! I couldn't imagine what they were thinking about the future. Yet this good-natured bunch of men were all trained to kill other people. How many of them would come back unhurt from this war?

There were always boys in the shipyard so no one took any notice of me. I soon fell into conversation with another boy called Nico. He was the same age as me but much smaller. He looked more like a boy of 13 than one who was almost 16.

"What do you do here at the Arsenale?" I asked him.

"I'm looking for a ship to take me on," Nico said.

He made it sound so easy!

"What do your family think?" I asked.

He just shrugged. "I haven't got a family," he said. "I'm an orphan. At least if they take me on board I know I'll get food every day."

That made me feel very ungrateful. I was always hungry but that wasn't because my parents didn't feed me. It was just because I was growing so fast.

Perhaps poor Nico was small because he never got enough to eat. But I knew from what the rowers said that the food on board ship would not be very good. Dry ship's biscuit, sometimes mixed with water to make a kind of biscuit soup! And almost never any meat.

I looked at the rowers' strong backs and arms and I knew they were going to this war only to win a pardon for their crimes and maybe to bring back some treasure.

The day I talked to Nico, I had a lot to think about on the way home. So much that I didn't even think of taking peaches. Perhaps it was also because the weather had changed and there was a cool breeze blowing so that I wasn't as hot and thirsty as usual.

I was walking across our square, my head down. I was thinking about Nico's confidence that a ship would take him on. And then a sweet voice said, "No peaches for me today, Signor?"

My mouth fell open in shock – Angelina had actually spoken to me!

I must have looked like an idiot as I babbled something about "not today". "But I can bring you some tomorrow," I said eagerly.

She smiled, and I saw she had the most charming dimples. And then her servant woman dragged her away, scolding her for speaking to "strange men".

4

Caught!

I was now like a person pulled in two directions by strong hands tugging at a rope. Half of me was sure I wanted to go and fight the Ottomans and, since I had met Nico, I was more confident that I would find a boat to take me on. The other half of me was full of wild dreams about Angelina – just because she had spoken to me and I had promised to bring her more fruit!

I was no use at all at work that next day. I got under everyone's feet and they gave me blows and curses. I couldn't focus on anything.

But I heard the talk and the excitement building around me and I picked up the sense that the fleet was getting ready to leave. Soon I would have to decide what to do.

"They say they haven't got nearly enough men," my father grumbled. "What's the point in us making such fine galleys if there's only a ragged crew to sail them?"

My father talked as if the carpenters were the only ones who made the galleys, but our work was just the first step in the process. When we had finished there were still masts and sails and many other parts to be added. Still, I understood what my father meant. A ship was nothing without its wooden keel to support it and its strong sides to keep the water out. And of course we built the firm decks the soldiers would stand on while they fought the Ottomans.

But surely, if they needed men, it would make it easier for me to get taken on board? Not that I was likely to be much use as a sailor. Or a soldier. Or a rower.

At last it struck me that I had been living my whole life as a dream up till now. I didn't know how to do anything except chop wood, light fires, fetch water and sweep wood shavings. Would any of these skills be any use on board a warship?

Or did that matter? I was strong enough and at least I was used to doing as I was told! And it was beginning to sound as if the commanders couldn't afford to be too fussy. There should be a place for a willing boy.

But was that what I really wanted? I was back to the old seesaw of my feelings for Angelina and my longing to go to sea and see the world.

When it was time for my break, I found Nico down by the water as usual. The sailors were getting used to him and I think they were beginning to know me too.

"Is it true?" I asked him. "Is it time for the fleet to leave?"

"Look around you," he said. "Everyone's so busy. I think it could be as soon as tomorrow."

Tomorrow! So I had very little time to decide. Nico looked so excited and happy that his mood made me feel I must choose the sea.

It was the longest day ever at work. I thought it would never end.

I still wasn't sure whether to take the plunge and go with the fleet the next day. If I packed a few things I could be back at the Arsenale at dawn and look for a ship to take me. But did I really want to take this big step now?

Then on the way home everything changed again.

I remembered my promise to Angelina and went to the usual wall with the overhanging fruit tree. But its branches were stripped of peaches. I wasn't the only hungry boy in Venice.

Almost without thinking, I set out to wander the streets in search of other free fruit.

In the end, I found myself in a part of the city I had never seen before. It was quiet, and there was no one about in the street. The houses here were tall and grand and several had gardens.

One garden had an apricot tree with branches full of fruit hanging over the wall. It was a very grand house indeed, and it was clear it must belong to one of the noble families of Venice.

But there were so few people to spot me that I soon had an armful of apricots. I tipped the wood shavings out of my bag and filled it with the fruit – they looked like little balls of pure sunshine.

What would it matter if my mother told me off for leaving the curls of wood behind? I might be leaving tomorrow in any case.

I got a bit carried away stuffing fruit into my bag. There was so much and no one else seemed to have spotted it. I'd have plenty to give my mother as well as Angelina.

And then a hand clamped itself on my wrist.

I yelped at the pain, and twisted to find myself looking into the eyes of a very angry young man.

He hadn't made a sound before he gripped my wrist but his face was white with fury. He was a nobleman, with a satin suit the same colour as the fruit I had stolen. In the few seconds before he spoke, I had taken all this in.

"You rat, you little thief!" he hissed. "Drop that bag."

I dropped it.

"What do you think you are doing, stealing from your betters?"

All the time he hung on to me with fingers as strong as the vice in my father's workshop. I had to grit my teeth in order not to cry with pain.

"I ... I am sorry, Signor," I babbled. "I didn't know. They were hanging over the wall –"

"You have enough there to set up your own fruit stall," he said. "Greedy as well as a thief."

He wouldn't have understood about Angelina, or my mother, or my own hunger. He looked like the sort of person who could eat fruit whenever he wanted.

"Please let me go," I said. "I won't do it again."

"No, you won't," he said, with a cruel smile. "It will be hard to steal anything ever again when your hands have been chopped off. I shall take you to the magistrates. That will teach you to steal from the Santo family."

Santo? But that was Angelina's name ...

And as if my thoughts could magic her up, all of a sudden she was there!

"Daniele!" she shouted. "What are you doing? That is Luca!"

I had a split second to realise that I had been stealing fruit for Angelina from her own garden before I realised that the young noble had released his grip.

That was all I needed. I ducked out from under his arm and ran as fast as I could.

My mind had been made up for me.

5

Runaway

I ran and ran until my breath rasped in my throat and I had to stop. I had no idea where I was. But I was so sore in my heart and body that I didn't care. My wrist really hurt and I kept thinking how much more it would have hurt to have my hand chopped off.

What a fool I had been!

But fear of the awful punishment was not so bad as the thought of what a stupid idiot I had been in front of Angelina. I groaned at the memory.

I guessed that the young man, Daniele, must be her older brother. And Angelina knew my name! She must have wanted to find it out. What would her brother think of the fact she knew a common thief? And, if he knew my name, could he track me down and have the terrible punishment carried out?

He had caught me red handed. And red handed I would be if the magistrates took an axe to my wrists. I cried out in fear and shame.

There was only one thing to do now. I couldn't hear the sound of running feet behind me so I was safe for maybe a few hours. I would have to find my way to the Arsenale and hide on one of the ships.

There was no time to say goodbye to my family or pack my few belongings. I would have to be taken on as a ship's boy just as I stood, with my workman's clothes stained with apricot juice.

My stomach rumbled, reminding me that I would miss supper at home. Goodness knows when I would get a meal again. Would it only be hard biscuit and water?

But what choice did I have? I was a wanted man now.

Little by little, my breathing slowed and I looked around me. I still didn't know where I was but in the distance I could see the tops of ships' masts. If I aimed for there I would get to the Arsenale.

But there is no such thing as a straight journey in Venice. You set off towards a point you can see and then you have to zigzag across little bridges to get over the canals.

My father once told me that the whole of Venice was a collection of tiny islands separated by water. And that was why you needed to know your way around the city.

After a while, the streets began to look familiar again and I soon knew where I was. And then I was at the Arsenale and found the gates locked!

Of course. What an idiot I was. I knew that the gates were chained and padlocked at night to stop thieves from getting in and stealing expensive bits of wood and metal.

I was very hungry and the sweat I had built up from running was cooling on my body, so I was beginning to feel cold too. It was getting dark and I was going to have a very uncomfortable night.

Just then the watchman came on his rounds, carrying a lighted torch.

He had his dog with him, a fierce hound called Bruno. I couldn't believe my luck!

At first Bruno barked to see someone at the gate, but as soon as he got my scent, he stopped and wagged his tail. I love dogs and I had often slipped Bruno a bit of cheese.

"Who is it?" the watchman said, and held up his torch. "Young Luca? What are you doing here at this hour of night?"

What lie could I think of?

"I have had a fight with my papa," I said.

It wasn't too far from the truth. My father would be furious when he found out that I'd run away. And why.

"I forgot the gates would be locked," I said. At least this *was* the truth. "I thought I could sleep in the workshop. And by tomorrow he might have calmed down."

Then I had another piece of luck. The watchman nodded in understanding. He had been a bit of a wild boy when he was young.

"I remember the fights I had with my papa – he had a terrible temper," he said. "Always best to keep out of his way until he had cooled down."

He unlocked the chain on the gates!

"Come on in, lad," he said. "Let me finish my rounds with Bruno and then you can come back to my hut for a bite of something hot. Then I'll unlock the workshop and you can sleep in there."

Everything had changed for the better. After a good meal of bread and stew – shared with the dog too – I lay down on a heap of sacks in the workshop and pulled more over me.

I can't say I slept much that night but I slept better than I would have done shivering up against the locked gates.

I vowed to myself that I would never forget the watchman's kindness. If I brought anything of value back from the battle, I would give him something.

Now all I had to worry about was finding a ship I could hide on.

At least it was a lot easier to think about with my stomach full of bread and meat and a cupful of red wine.

Whatever the morning would bring, I could face it now.

6

A Willing Boy

I must have slept a bit because I had a dream about apricots. When I stumbled out of the workshop, rubbing my eyes, I thought I must still be half asleep, because I still saw apricot – the colour.

Then I was wide awake! It was Daniele Santo, Angelina's brother. The apricot colour was his cloak. He was talking to another man down by the water.

What was Santo doing in here? There was only one reason I could think of – he must have found out from Angelina where I worked. How much had she found out about me? I had to get down to the water myself and find a galley to hide in. There was no time to seek out a captain and ask for a place.

With great care, I sneaked round the back ways of the vast yard, which was beginning to stir with workers.

Nico had been right. There was a line of elegant galleys ready to launch into the water. I think some had already left.

There was one sitting in the water, just getting ready to cast off. In all the noise and crush of sailors and soldiers getting aboard, I spotted Nico on the deck.

I waved and called his name but he didn't hear me. It was a beautiful ship. And if I could get on board, I would have one friend to look out for me.

I looked at the name in gold letters on the side of the ship – *L'Angelo*. *The Angel*!

I thought of the lovely Angelina and my mind was made up. It was a sign.

There was such a crowd of men walking up the gangway on to the ship that it was easier than I had dared hope just to walk aboard.

Someone did shout, "Where's your pack?" but I got swept up in the crowd before I had to answer.

I should have felt pleased. This was what I had wanted – to leave Venice and have adventures at sea. But it was never supposed to be this way. I had no belongings other than the clothes I stood up in. And I knew that the law was after me.

The horrible thought came into my mind that I could never go back. A huge wave of homesickness washed over me, even before *The Angel* had left the Lagoon!

I tried to make myself invisible and keep out of people's way, but everyone on board seemed to have a job to do and a place to be. And some breakfast inside them, I thought, as the memory of last night's supper faded.

"Luca!"

There at last was a friendly face. "Nico!" I said. "I am so glad to see you."

"You're on *The Angel* too!" Nico said. "But where is your stuff?"

"I don't have any stuff. I had to run away." And I told him everything that had happened.

While we talked, the planks below our feet started to move. I nearly fell over – the galley was setting out to sea.

The rowers strained their backs and arms as they pulled at the long wooden oars and moved the galley out of the yard and into the Lagoon.

"Where are we going?" I asked Nico. I had never been so glad to have a friend.

"You haven't thought very hard about this, have you?" he said. "We're going to sail down to Sicily, where we'll meet up with the rest of the fleet."

"And then?" I asked.

"And then to battle!"

It was really going to happen!

"Um, Nico – do they feed boys on this ship?" I asked.

Nico grinned and took a hunk of bread out of his bag and gave it to me.

"Here, eat this," he said. "Yes, they'll feed us but it won't be fine dining."

I didn't mind – at least I still had two hands to hold my chunk of bread with.

As we headed for the open sea my mood was a strange mix of wild excitement and terror at the huge step I had taken.

I might have both my hands still, but what if an Ottoman attacked me with his sword? Who knows what might get cut off or whether I would even survive the battle?

I pushed those thoughts down as well as I could and focused on the odd feeling of gliding across the water.

The rowers had got up a steady rhythm now and we were making good progress. At last everyone was getting sorted out on deck.

"That's the Captain," Nico said. He pointed to a tall man with a black beard. "Giovanni Angelo."

The Captain looked as if he'd been at sea all his life.

"The same name as his ship?" I asked. "That's lucky."

The Captain moved with swift steps among the sailors and soldiers, sending everyone to their right places.

At last he got to us.

"Nico," he said. "I know you, but who is your friend? I don't remember taking on *two* ragged boys in Venice."

He smiled as he said it and I decided I liked him.

"I am Luca, Sir," I said. "A friend of Nico's."

"How old are you?" he asked.

"16," I said. "And I am willing to do whatever you need. I'm strong enough – look!"

I flexed my arms, to show him.

The Captain laughed. "You might regret that promise before you see Venice again," he said. "But I like a willing boy. You are welcome aboard."

And that was that. I was now a member of *The Angel*'s company of men and I had never felt prouder. The Captain obviously hadn't heard that I was a thief and a runaway.

The Captain got the quartermaster to add my name to a list he was making of everyone on board.

The quartermaster scratched my name on a little slip of ivory and gave it to me. "Keep it safe," he said gruffly. "You'll get no food without it."

So I would get fed! He also told me I was the only Luca on *The Angel*, so he didn't need to know my family name.

Nico took me down into the hold of the ship and we found a little corner where we put the two mats we'd been given.

I crawled on to mine and before I knew it, I was fast asleep, rocked by the movement of the ship across the waves.

7

The Angel's Man

I woke up a few hours later with a horrible feeling in my stomach. I had to run to the deck and throw up over the side.

There were cheers and laughter from the men on board, but as the days went by I was relieved to find I wasn't the only one who suffered from sea-sickness. Not the rowers and not the crew – they were all too used to the sea. And not Nico – which was annoying even though he was very kind to me. But several of the soldiers, young and old, spent as much time hanging over the ship's rails as I did, casting their stomach contents into the waves. Not that there was much to get rid of since I couldn't eat anything. And to think I'd been worried I wouldn't be fed!

On the third day my stomach calmed down and I felt hungry for the first time since we left Venice. I ate some dry biscuit and it tasted pretty good.

"Right, men!" the Captain said. "You've all found your sea legs now. It's a good thing we've had this voyage to Sicily to help get you used to life at sea. You've got to be fit to fight the Ottomans."

For the first time for days I saw that we were still in sight of the shore. We must be travelling along the coast all the way down south to Sicily.

It was a lot hotter here. I saw that all the men who had gathered round to listen to the Captain looked a lot better than they had before. So they had all found their sea legs.

"From now on," the Captain went on, "I want you up on deck every morning for drills and exercises. We'll start tomorrow. I don't want to give the rest of the fleet any reason to make fun of *The Angel*'s men."

So I was one of *The Angel*'s men! I liked that. And now that I felt so much better in my body, my spirits rose too. I was getting used to my new home – a home that was always on the move and was made of almost nothing but wood.

At first it had been very confusing. There were so many men – over two hundred, I reckoned – living in a really small space. But as the days went by and I began to notice the patterns of life on board, I could see that everyone knew what to do and where to be at any time.

And I got very good at keeping out of people's way.

Everyone had an important job to do except Nico and me. But we turned up on deck early each morning for the exercises and drills. I thought I could already see my muscles growing bigger.

The rumour went round that we were near Sicily, where we were going to meet the rest of the fleet in the stretch of water between the island and the mainland.

"Then do you think we'll be off to meet the Ottoman fleet?" I asked Nico.

"I don't think we'll go right away," he said. "I think all the commanders have to get together and decide what to do."

"So maybe we'll get to go ashore?" I said.

"Maybe."

I was feeling very cheerful, with the sun on my back and the hope of a few days on land. War with the Ottomans still seemed very far away and I was able to forget about it for hours on end.

And then I saw him.

My enemy – Daniele Santo – was on board the same ship as me!

I don't know why I hadn't seen him before. Perhaps the gentlemen-soldiers had their own area on the ship, and maybe he had been even more seasick than me. But here he was now, his apricot-coloured cloak thrown off in the heat.

All my cheerfulness disappeared like a puddle in the sun. This was a much worse danger than the Ottomans because it was much closer. I didn't know if he could carry out his threats while we were at sea but I knew from now on I would have to be very careful.

I told Nico and he offered to cut my hair for me. That was a brilliant idea! My face was already darkened by the sun and I had been given two blue jackets and pairs of trousers to wear as an *Angel's* man. It was only my long blond hair – unusual in Venice – that might give me away.

It was a good job I had no mirror to see the result.

Nico was a wonderful friend, but no barber – he hacked at my curls with his knife until I could feel a short ragged edge round my neck and a messy fringe fell over my eyes.

At least I felt a bit less like the apricot thief that Daniele had caught in the act. With luck he would never recognise me. But I intended to keep out of his way all the same.

Then I saw the fleet – and I forgot about Daniele.

For all that I had been brought up in the Lagoon city and worked in the Arsenale for years, I had never seen so many galleys in one place.

The tall masts filled the horizon. There were about a hundred galleys, and Nico said they came from Spain.

"How do you know so much about everything?" I asked him.

He just shrugged. "I listen to what people say," he said. "I always have."

The pilot of our ship was guiding *The Angel* into a gap in the water. For the rest of the day we saw other galleys arrive from Venice. We could tell by their flags.

I had no idea there were going to be so many!

For the first time since I'd scrambled aboard *The Angel*, I realised what it was to be part of a full fleet that was about to go to war.

8

A Storm

There must have been about two hundred ships in that stretch of water. I kept trying to count them but I always came up with a different number. It felt as if you could step from deck to deck and reach the island of Sicily on one side or the very tip of Italy on the other.

Our Captain went in a small boat with his top officers to meet the Captain General of the whole fleet on his ship, *The Real*.

And yes, I had to ask Nico who the Captain General was – I really didn't know enough about any of this.

"He's called Don John," Nico said. "His father was the old Emperor Charles. His brother is King Philip of Spain – well, his half-brother."

"So is Philip the Emperor now?" I had a very hazy idea about politics.

"No," Nico said. "That's Maximilian. The old Emperor wasn't married to Don John's mother, so Don John couldn't be Emperor. But he's a good soldier they say, for all he's only 24."

It seemed that Don John had to have lots of meetings with the ships' captains before anything happened. And we *Angel*'s men had nothing to do but keep the decks scrubbed and keep ourselves busy with exercises.

At least we were close to land and could get fresh supplies of food and water. After a few days, some of the men were allowed on shore – only the soldiers at first. I watched with relief as Daniele Santo set off in a small boat for a night on the town in Messina.

I felt I could breathe freely for the first time since I'd seen him on board.

I sat on a coil of rope and let myself daydream about Angelina. I was sure she had wanted to save me on that dreadful last day in Venice. Did that mean she liked me? But now I was finding it difficult to imagine her face. I kept seeing Fina's instead. But then I had known her much longer.

I really missed Fina and I wondered if she ever thought about me. Before Nico she had been my only friend, and she was good at cheering me up. She would probably have laughed at my fears about Daniele.

"What makes you think you're so easy to remember?" she might say. "I bet he's forgotten you already."

Then I heard the Captain talking and I forgot all about my daydreams. I was going to be like Nico and learn things by listening.

"The galleasses will be here soon," Captain Angelo was saying.

"And then we can set out?" the other man asked.

There was a heavy sigh from Captain Angelo. "I hope so but it's taking a long time for all the commanders to agree."

"The weather won't hold if we wait much longer," the other man said. "If we don't leave soon, it will be too late to fight the Ottomans at sea."

"I know," the Captain said. "We need a decision fast."

I didn't know who or what a galleass was. Was it another sort of galley? But I understood the need for action soon. Every autumn the Mediterranean Sea had terrible storms, which reached us in Venice too. If we waited much longer, we wouldn't be able to sail to meet the Ottoman fleet, wherever it was waiting for us. And then what would we do?

I was glad that such decisions weren't made by ship's boys like me! But I could hear the worry in our Captain's voice.

I went to find Nico and asked him about the galleasses.

For once, he wasn't such a mine of information.

"I think they're a kind of gunship," he said.

A crew member had been listening to us. "They're more than that," he said. "They're big merchant galleys with serious gun power. There are six coming down from Venice. We won't leave till they're here."

*

So August turned into September. I was getting bored waiting for the battle – what a fool I was then!

Then the six galleasses arrived. They were enormous, with five men on each oar, and full of guns.

'At last,' I thought. 'We can be on our way.'

Then the storm struck.

After the heat we had been suffering, it should have been a relief. But the rain was solid for three days and all of us were like drowned rats, except for the gentlemen-soldiers who had a nice dry cabin.

On the first day of the storm, I found Nico curled up in a ball on his sleeping mat. He was shaking and his eyes were tight shut.

"What's the matter?" I asked. "Are you ill?"

"Th-thunder," he stammered. "I'm scared."

He looked terrible – white as a new sail and shivering like someone with the plague.

I didn't understand. I thought thunder and lightning were rather exciting but I could see Nico wasn't faking.

"It's OK," I said. "It won't hurt you."

But I couldn't help him. He stayed like that the whole three days, till the wind dropped and the storm was over. I wondered if it was the noise that scared him and how he would cope under fire in the battle.

We were all in a terrible state by then. The men hadn't been able to exercise on the sopping wet deck and we were all bad-tempered and picking fights with each other.

But it felt wonderful to feel the sun shining on my face again. I dried out my spare jacket and trousers on a coil of rope and soon I had something dry to wear again.

Even Nico was back to his usual self.

I was a bit worried that we wouldn't set out at all now the storms had started and that the battle just wouldn't happen.

But the day after the storm stopped there was a big meeting of all the commanders and our

Captain came back to *The Angel* with a wooden chest.

We wondered what was in it as all of us were called up on deck.

"A present from Don John!" Captain Angelo said. "One for each of you." He took out what looked like strings of beads.

Nico and I were last to get our present – it was a rosary to help us say our prayers.

It was the first time since I left Venice that I had anything to call my own.

"What does it mean?" I asked Nico.

Our Captain overheard me. "It means, my boy, that we are going to war! Get ready, men. The fleet leaves tomorrow."

9

Fighting in the Fleet

To my great relief, I wasn't seasick any more. I got used to the movement of the boards under my feet and I ran about as neat on my feet as I was on land.

There was a lot of running about to do. Now that *The Angel* was surging through the waves towards battle there were more drills than ever. Our Captain made sure that Nico and I knew where the gunpowder for the great cannons was stored, and the stocks of shot for the soldiers' weapons.

"When we are in the thick of the battle," he said, "you will have to run across decks slippery with water and blood. You must get everything to the soldiers and the gun crews before they even know they need you."

We practised hard, running from the gunpowder stores in the hold up to the big guns on deck. But I knew it would be very different when we were under fire.

There were still days when I wondered if we ever would be under fire – the storms hadn't finished with us yet and I got several good drenchings on my first voyage out into the open Mediterranean.

I saw Daniele Santo many times and he saw me but he showed no sign that he knew who I was. In fact, none of the fighting men took any notice of us boys. We were just like bits of rigging to them.

I wondered if they all knew how to fight. Some were professional soldiers who had seen a lot of battles. But others were just nobles with swords and muskets who had taken it into their heads to go and help their city, for glory – or maybe for plunder.

How much use were they going to be in a battle?

I kept thinking about Daniele Santo. I knew nothing about him except that his grip was fierce. Every time I saw him I couldn't help looking down at my hands and remembering what he had threatened. What would I do if I had to fetch bullets for his musket?

The thrill of the fact that I was on board a ship on its way to a battle helped to take my mind off these thoughts. Every time I looked out to sea and saw the rest of the fleet, I could feel a stupid grin spreading across my face. Two hundred galleys! And the six heavy galleasses with their weight of guns – about forty each – and five men to an oar.

We had only three men to each oar on *The Angel* and I knew we were seriously short of men. But if I'd known how they would increase our numbers I'd have been happy to stick with our limited manpower.

After about ten days – I lost count – we had left the "foot" of Italy behind us and I could see another coast ahead.

I asked one of the sailors what it was.

"Corfu," he said.

One of Venice's islands! I wondered if it was already in the hands of the Ottomans and my heart beat faster. If they'd captured the island then that's where our battle would be.

I could see no enemy fleet.

Don John ordered our fleet to anchor and again the ship's captains went off to meet their commanders on the island.

Captain Angelo looked grim when he came back on board.

"The Ottomans have gone," he said. "They raided the island and sailed south. Their fleet is going to spend the winter at Lepanto."

Lepanto! That was the first time I'd ever heard that name and it sent chills down my spine. I had no idea where it was, but somehow I knew it was part of my destiny.

"Don John himself is coming to inspect all the galleys," the Captain said. "So you'd better have *The Angel* looking ship-shape!"

We scrubbed till the decks shone and our hands were red, and when Don John came on board our ship there was no fault to be found. But he frowned when the Captain showed him the list of *The Angel*'s men.

"I'll send you some of the Spanish," he told the Captain. "I want to even out the numbers so that all the galleys have the same amount of soldiers."

The Captain didn't look happy but he nodded in agreement.

Later we heard that Don John had gone so far as to condemn four galleys from Venice as unfit to go to sea! Four of our ships would go back to the Lagoon with their tails between their legs. What a humiliation!

Better to accept some Spanish soldiers to join our crew than be sent back home and miss the battle.

At least, that's what I thought at first. Then the new soldiers arrived – they were Spanish, and a few Italians who were not from Venice, and they were not at all happy. They were used to their own ships and their own captains and commanders and they didn't want to be on *The Angel* any more than our soldiers wanted them to be there.

The first fight broke out that very evening. There was a row over sleeping space, insults about mothers and girlfriends, and before you knew it the deck of *The Angel* was full of men with guns and daggers and our senior officers had to pull them apart.

"Have you all gone mad?" the Captain shouted. "There's a whole fleet of Ottomans waiting for us in the port of Lepanto and all you can do is fight among yourselves!"

Nico and I kept our heads down and stayed out of the way of the glaring, staring soldiers. But later we heard it had been the same on every ship where Don John had sent new men.

On one galley it was so bad that it turned into a full-scale riot.

"Don John will have to do something," Nico said. "Or the whole fleet will collapse and there won't be any battle."

But it was the Captain General from Venice, Sebastian Venier, who stopped the riot – at least to start with. On the ship where the fighting was worst, Venier ordered that a Spanish officer was to be strung up to the yardarm and hanged.

I had never seen a man killed before. I watched his arms and legs jerk as he swung in the air. Then, as soon as he was still, I ran to the other side of the ship and hurled my supper up over the rail, just as sick as when we first took to sea.

Was this how it was all going to end? Would our fleet tear itself apart before we ever saw an Ottoman?

10

A Horrible Death

Well, all hell broke loose after the hanging. There were riots on all the ships I could see. The Spanish fought the men of Venice, and we fought other Italians.

This wasn't just scrapping of the kind I'd seen when men were bored and perhaps had too much to drink. That was fist fighting, but here men drew their weapons and got ready to massacre each other.

It was then that I found out what a great leader Don John was. He went from ship to ship convincing the soldiers that they were not each other's enemy and that they must save their hatred for the Ottomans.

What really swung their mood was that Don John sacked Venier as Captain General of the

Venice ships and named a man called Barberigo as the representative for our fleet in all his War Councils. And another officer went round and soothed the tempers of the men.

"Don John is a real diplomat," Nico said. "The sort of man who can walk into a bar and all the fighting stops."

I believed him, even if it didn't seem very likely to me that Nico had ever been in a bar. Or a fight, come to that.

I was glad when I heard that Barberigo was going to be in charge of the Left Wing of the battle plan of our Alliance, because *The Angel* was going to be on that wing.

I was perhaps just a bit disappointed that I wouldn't be right in the middle, with the dashing Don John. But everything I heard about the line-up for the battle made it all seem so much more real.

In a few days we were back at sea and on the way to Corinth. I was further from home than I had ever been and for the first time I passed the shore of a country that was not my own.

Not that I saw much of it, since a heavy fog came down over the sea. Our ships pulled into harbour and I was amazed that our pilot could even find his way in all that foul mist.

Then we waited. I knew we must be very near the Ottoman fleet now.

The soldiers had grown used to the new conditions and for all they still grumbled about having to serve together, they were no longer drawing swords and loading muskets.

And then we heard news so dreadful that all the quarrels between our men were forgotten.

We knew that the Ottomans had attacked Cyprus. There had been a long siege – ten months – and then the Governor of the main port of the island had to give in. He had run out of food and gunpowder, so he met the Ottomans to discuss terms of surrender.

But the Ottoman leader had betrayed the terms. The Ottomans had killed everyone – except the Governor. The Governor was tortured for days. They cut off his ears and his nose.

As soon as I heard this I clapped my hands over my own ears, remembering my mother's threats.

But that wasn't all.

They had skinned him alive.

What a horrible way to die. I had to rush to the side of the galley again when I heard about it.

"People always say things like that about the enemy," Nico told me, to try to cheer me up.

But it seemed that this time it was no gory tale told to make us hate our enemies more.

Captain Angelo called us all up on deck and confirmed the news.

"The Governor has two kinsmen in our fleet," he said. "They command the two galleasses on the left wing. That is where we, *The Angel*'s men, will fight under Barberigo's command. They want to avenge his horrible death," the Captain went on. "And it will be up to us to help them. If ever your courage fails, think of what they did to the Governor, that brave son of Venice, and let your anger help you."

I didn't think I'd have any problem with that, the way I was feeling now.

I looked around me and saw the same anger on every man's face – even Daniele's, where he stood near the Captain.

I knew that every man in the fleet felt a cold fury in their blood, which would turn into hot rage when we came face to face with the Ottomans.

It seemed that would happen very soon if the awful fog lifted.

Eight fast galleys were sent on ahead to Lepanto to check where the Ottoman fleet was.

We all knew that the battle was likely to happen within the next week. But none of us knew just how soon it would be.

As we set out again in the cold dawn, we thought we still had several days to prepare. We were wrong.

The two fleets would meet the very next day.

11

"Conquer or Die!"

That night I fell into a deep sleep which was full of fog. Out of the mists came the elegant figure of Angelina Santo and I stretched my arms out to her. Then her beautiful face changed into that of an Ottoman holding a dagger.

The Ottoman gave a terrible cry and launched himself at me.

"I'll skin you alive!" he said, and he slipped his dagger under my arm. It was when I saw the skin fall from my arm like the peel from an apple that I screamed myself awake.

"Can't you keep it down, boy?" one of the sailors grumbled. "Some of us have a battle to fight soon. We need our beauty sleep!"

I sat up, tangled in my blanket and soaked in sweat. I touched my arm and found my skin unharmed.

As I lay back down, I thought that hiding away on *The Angel* had been the worst mistake I had ever made in my life.

Things looked better as we got ready to pull away from the place near Ithaca where we had rested in the early dawn. It was always better when we were on the move and I didn't have time to think.

It was a Sunday and we started the day with Mass, taken by the galley's chaplain.

Then the bosun walked up and down the deck with a whip and blew on a silver whistle to get everyone in place.

That was when I realised that the battle was really going to happen today.

All the Venice galleys were putting up yellow flags. There were nearly forty of us on the left flank, all moving in line together, and it would help the pilots keep a straight line when we got there if they could keep their eyes on these flags.

In spite of my fear, my heart swelled with pride at being a part – even a tiny part – of the massive fleet of the Holy Alliance.

We didn't spot the Ottoman fleet until half past seven in the morning. We were shocked to see they had as many galleys as our side did.

An uncanny silence fell over all our ships. We had jobs to do and got on with them. I was put to clearing the decks, along with Nico, and even we didn't dare speak.

Some of the crew came along and struck the chains off the rowers who were not free men and were chained to their oars. Then they were given weapons so that they could fight when the two fleets clashed.

"I bet the Ottoman galley slaves don't get released," Nico whispered. "They'll go down with their ships if their galleys are sunk."

I watched as they towed the six heavy galleasses out in front of our fleet until they were about a mile ahead of us. The captains of the two in front of our left flank were the kinsman of the Governor who had been skinned by the Ottomans. I could only imagine what was going through their minds as they faced the enemy.

Then orders came to take the wooden rams off the front of each galley. It was to make room for our main guns.

All of a sudden I saw a light frigate speed along in front of the galleys. A splendid figure stood up in it. It was Don John! He was checking that our line was straight. He was in shiny gold armour and he carried a holy cross, which he held up high for us all to see.

"The time for fighting has come!" he shouted up to us. "We are here to conquer or die! There is no Heaven for cowards."

As if his words had made it happen, the wind changed and all our sails were filled. We were so close to the Ottoman fleet we could see the enemy on board. They seemed to be dancing! I could hear the sound of drums and flutes and I could see a green and gold banner flying from their flagship.

By then it was about ten o'clock in the morning.

Don John was back on his galley, *The Real*, and his men shook out a great banner with a giant cross on it. I saw that every ship on our side was raising their own holy cross.

Then the galleasses fired their great guns. The noise made us deaf. I couldn't hear the Ottoman music any more and I bet they had stopped dancing. But we were too far away for the cannonballs to do anything but land in the sea without doing any harm. It was just a warning.

Men stood on our deck with a rosary in one hand and a weapon in the other – a musket, a sword or a bow. I thought I could make out Daniele Santo on the far side of the deck from me.

I clutched my own rosary.

The enemy were so close now that I could see that *The Real* was sailing straight at the Ottoman flagship. I wondered what its name might be, but I couldn't read the letters written on its prow.

The galleasses fired again and now we were close enough for them to hit an Ottoman galley. They hit it below the waterline and very quickly it began to sink.

A huge cheer went up from our fleet – we had claimed the first strike!

But as I watched the Ottoman galley sink below the water I thought of the chained slaves at the oars who would now be drowning, and I felt sick again.

That was the last time I thought of anything clearly.

I was in my first battle and from then on everything was chaos.

12

The Battle of Lepanto

I saw the Ottoman galleys on the flank opposite us heading for our galleasses. They wanted revenge for their lost ship.

But the men on the galleasses just kept firing and the Ottoman oars flew into the air in splinters. I saw one of the galleasses make a slow turn so that it would be easier for her to fire on the Ottoman galleys that were besetting her. After that there was no time to watch what was going on.

It was still only about ten minutes since the first shot and now the Ottoman ships were upon us.

The noise as the two sets of galleys crashed against each other was like nothing I had ever heard – wood and metal and men screaming.

I think every man on *The Angel* fell to the deck when the enemy ship smashed into us. Every man scrambled to his feet and screamed as he launched himself at the Ottomans in the fierce fight that would decide whether we were boarding their ship or they were coming on to ours.

It was too late for cannon fire then. It was just a mess of musket fire, flashing swords and arrows.

The sky was dark with arrows and the air thick with smoke from the muskets. My job was to make sure the soldiers had powder and shot, but as I darted back and forth across the deck I slipped on blood and stumbled over bodies.

There were Italian and Ottoman corpses and – worse – men who were not dead but horribly wounded. Soon there were guts spilled on the deck and severed limbs as well as blood.

It was a scene from Hell.

I didn't know which of us boarded the other's ship first as there was close fighting on both decks. Battles sound so neat and organised when they are in the past and people describe them. I can tell you that when you are in one, it's not a bit like that.

No words can describe the smells – blood and guts and gunpowder and shit – or the sound of men's screams as they die or are horribly mutilated.

I could think of only two things – getting shot to the soldiers who needed it, and staying alive.

What I really wanted to do was to go and hide below deck, but I was too ashamed to be such a coward. All around me men from Italy and Spain were fighting shoulder to shoulder, bravely facing the enemy.

The fighting seemed to go on for ever. I found out later it was only three or four hours.

On one of my mad dashes for more shot, I ran into Nico.

"They say Barberigo's been killed," he gasped. "Shot in the eye by an enemy arrow."

The Commander of our flank! This was a terrible blow. If a commander in armour could be killed by an arrow, how much more dangerous must it be for a boy in a canvas shirt and trousers?

"How horrible!" I said. "Take care, Nico."

It was the last thing I ever said to him.

As Nico scuttled across the deck with his arms full of shot, I saw his body shoot up into the air. A stray musket ball from the Ottomans had caught him and cut short his life in an instant.

I was numb with shock.

Then I heard someone shouting for more shot and I realised that with Nico gone I'd have to work twice as hard.

I picked up all the shot he had let fall and ran. There wasn't even time to say goodbye or close his eyes.

I dodged arrows and musket balls as I ran to where the fighting was at its fiercest. To my horror, the first soldier I saw was Daniele Santo. But he was too busy firing on the Ottomans to take any notice of me.

The fighting was so intense that I had to fall to the deck and crawl between the soldiers' legs. I wanted to stay hidden. It was madness because it wasn't any safer down on the deck.

A thud beside me brought me to my senses. It was an Ottoman – or at least, it had been.

Now it was just another body, a man with a bullet hole in the middle of his forehead.

I couldn't remember why I was here, why Italy and Spain were fighting the Ottomans. This body, still warm, with blood leaking out of its mouth, had been a man just the same as his enemies. A man like the one Nico could have grown up to be, if he hadn't just been killed.

In that moment, I just wanted it all to stop.

I didn't much care whether it ended with my death or not. I didn't want to see any more people killing or being killed.

I took a deep breath and scuttled back to the store for another armful of shot.

I closed my eyes as I went past Nico's body.

Back again with the shot to the soldiers fighting the Ottomans.

There were more of the enemy swarming on to *The Angel* now. A large Ottoman with a beard leaped into the crush of bodies waving his sword.

It was all so fast. I can't really say what happened next. I saw the Ottoman, with his sword arm raised high. I saw a blur of apricot satin and heard a musket fail to fire.

I threw myself at the apricot colour and pulled the soldier down just as the Ottoman's sword whistled through the air.

And then everything went black and the battle was over for me.

13

Daniele Santo

The voices came from very far off.

"He'll have to lose that hand."

"There's nothing else we can do for him."

"Such a tragedy for a young man."

"He'll die if we don't amputate."

I was having one of my worst nightmares. They were going to cut off my hand and I couldn't stop them. I couldn't get any words out of my mouth. My tongue seemed to have swelled to fill my mouth and I couldn't say anything.

I wanted to scream, "But it was only some apricots!"

I wondered where I was and whether this was about stealing fruit or facing an Ottoman with a sword.

Was I asleep? My eyes were closed and it was dark but I heard the creaking of wood and felt the movement of the sea under me. Was I on *The Angel* or back in Venice?

I heard the sickening sound of a blade cutting through a joint and I smelled hot tar.

Then I realised I couldn't feel anything and I fainted.

How much later was it when I opened my eyes at last and realised that I really was awake?

I was lying below deck but not on my sleeping mat. I was on a bunk in the surgeon's cabin. As soon as I realised this, I looked down at my hands.

They were both there! I flexed them into fists – they seemed to be working as normal. Little by little, I checked over my whole body. Apart from a throbbing pain in my head, I seemed to be unharmed and unmarked.

There was a groan from the bunk next to me. I looked over and the movement made my head feel much worse. There was a man stretched out on the bunk, with his right arm wrapped in bandages that were stained with blood.

The ship's surgeon came in.

"Ah, you are both awake!" he said. "Good."

He felt the other patient's head. "You are going to be all right, Sir," he said.

Sir? Was it one of the officers? Or a nobleman?

The surgeon moved to one side and I saw a flash of apricot-coloured cloth.

It was Daniele Santo.

He was struggling to sit up. The surgeon propped him with pillows and he looked over at me.

"Luca!" he said. "It's you, isn't it?"

How did he know my name? Oh yes, Angelina must have told him. I could see he looked a bit like her – the same reddish gold hair and blue eyes. Maybe his whole family looked like angels?

He tried to reach out towards me but then he realised his arm was useless.

Was he going to tell the surgeon I was a thief?

"Thank you," he said, and fell back on the pillows.

That was the last thing I expected!

"You owe your life to Luca," the surgeon said.

"I know," said Daniele. "I remember."

Well, I didn't remember. I thought I must be dreaming again. Here was my worst enemy – and he was thanking me for saving his life.

"How are you feeling, Luca?" the surgeon asked me. "You hit your head hard when you pulled Signor Santo out of the way of that Ottoman. You fell on the deck with the Signor on top of you."

The Ottoman. The one with the sword.

"What happened to him?" I managed to ask. "The Ottoman?"

"I shot him," a voice said from the doorway. It was Captain Angelo.

All of a sudden, I wondered if the battle was still going on.

"The Ottomans," I said. "The battle … What time is it?"

The Captain came over to look at us both. I could see now that there were other bodies on bunks in this cabin, but some were very still.

"It's evening," the Captain said. He looked terribly tired and there was blood on his face. "We won. The Ottoman fleet has been defeated."

"Have we suffered many losses?" Daniele asked.

"Many," said the Captain. He sat down on the end of my bunk and put his head in his hands. "So much loss of life on both sides. It's hard to feel we have had a victory."

I thought of Nico, my friend, and the tears came.

"What happens to the bodies?" I asked.

"The Ottomans have been thrown overboard," the Captain said.

I thought of the big man who had attacked Daniele.

"Our own men?" I asked.

"We have said a service over their bodies and lowered them into the sea, with their rosaries round their fingers," the Captain said.

So, it didn't make much difference, I thought. All the bodies ended up in the water – Nico and the Ottoman were both food for fishes.

"But you are one of the heroes of the day," the Captain was saying. And he smiled, not at the noble young soldier, Daniele, but at me – the most junior member of the crew.

"You will be rewarded when we get back to Venice," the Captain said. "You saved this young noble's life, without any thought for your own safety. I saw it all happen."

I couldn't get my poor sore head round it. I had been afraid of being a thief, hunted by the law, but I was going to be treated as a hero.

When the Captain left, Daniele turned to me. "My sister explained about the fruit – that you were taking it for her," he said. "I tried to find you at the Arsenale but I had no idea you were on board *The Angel*. You look different."

"So you won't tell anyone I was stealing?" I asked.

"No. You can come and take fruit from our garden any time you want."

"I'm sorry about your hand," I said.

Daniele held up his bandaged arm. "Me too," he said. "But you know, if you hadn't pulled me out of the way, that Ottoman's sword would have gone through my head, not my hand."

I thought he was being very brave. But as he lay back down I saw the glitter of tears in his eyes.

14

After the Battle

By the evening my head was much better and the surgeon ordered me to go up on deck.

"It will do you good to get some fresh air," he told me.

It was a bit more than that! The weather had turned and there was a blustery cold wind blowing.

The water was full of floating bodies and bits of broken ships. I didn't want to look closely. I hoped that Nico's body had been weighted down before he was cast over the side.

On the shore there were burning ships and someone told me they were the galleys from our side that were too damaged to sail again. They had been set on fire and were now just blackened hulks. *The Angel* had pulled into shore at a port near the burning galleys, along with all the rest of the fleet.

I looked around *The Angel* and realised she had escaped any serious damage. She had been a lucky ship for me. All of a sudden, I began to shiver.

"That's enough air," said the surgeon, who had come to find me. "Get back down below and wrap yourself in the extra blankets I've put on your bunk."

I was happy to leave those sad sights but as I went back below deck I realised there was something else different. The oarsmen were all Ottomans now – they must be prisoners of war because they were chained to the oars.

Next morning I stepped on to dry land for the first time since I had left Venice.

In an instant, my legs gave way under me. I would have fallen if a sailor hadn't grabbed me under the arms. They were all laughing at me – but in a kind way. I had become a bit of a mascot to the crew of *The Angel*. More than one of them had come to say they were sorry about poor Nico.

Everyone was in such a good mood – even the ones with wounds – because they had survived the battle.

Of course, some had lost friends but the general mood was really happy and I began to share it. After all, here I was alive, with nothing worse than a bang to the head.

We had got rich plunder from the Ottoman galleys. Nearly two hundred of them had been destroyed or sunk. As well as their galley slaves we had taken all their food. The cooks were burning fires along the shore and boiling up rice and beans from the barrels that we had saved from the Ottoman ships.

It was turning into a cross between a party and a wake.

We drank to lost friends.

Stories were flying round our camp. They said we had killed 25,000 Ottomans but only 7,000 of our men had died. It still seemed like an awful lot of corpses to me. From the sound of men groaning, I thought there would be plenty more dead of their wounds before we could get home to Venice.

As the day wore on, it was hard to stay cheerful with all the groans – and the awful weather that had struck us. We were lucky the battle hadn't been a day later.

I was glad to get back on board and into the surgeon's warm cabin.

"One more night," he told me. "And then you can go back to your old sleeping mat. I need these bunks for the wounded."

Daniele would stay longer, I knew. His wound might be followed by a fever – that was always the worry after a battle.

The next day we were on the move again. In spite of the terrible weather, Don John had decided we must head back to Corfu.

That was the most miserable two weeks of my whole life. The fleet moved slowly, and more men died every day. I got used to the sound of sailors heaving bodies overboard into the water. And the weather didn't get any better, so I was cold and wet most of the time. We were running out of food too. I missed Nico's cheerful company, and now that he had gone I had no real friend to talk to. I thought more and more often about Fina.

There was not much for me to do. Every day I visited Daniele in the surgeon's cabin. Not all the wounded were lucky enough to be kept there – there were too many of them. I realised I had got special treatment for a couple of days because I had saved Daniele from the Ottoman.

We talked about Daniele's home and his family, and of course about his sister, the beautiful Angelina. I watched him every day to see if he was getting a fever but he remained well. His arm must have hurt a lot but he didn't complain.

"I'm going to ask a carpenter to make me a wooden hand when we get back to Venice," he said. "Do you think your father would do it?"

"Carving a hand is a bit different from making the keel for a ship," I said. "But we can ask him."

As we were tossed about on the stormy sea, I simply couldn't imagine ever being in my father's workshop again. Would he even be pleased to see me? I had just run off to sea without any word to my family.

My welcome home wouldn't be like Daniele's. His parents had known he was enlisting to fight the Ottomans, like so many other young nobles in Venice. And many of them would never come home.

Daniele was worried about his mother and sister. "They will be so upset about my hand," he said. "And I won't be able to fight in any more battles."

"Let's hope there are no more to fight in," I said.

"If I am no good in war, maybe I won't be any better off in love," Daniele said. "Have you ever been in love, Luca? Do you think any woman will want to marry a man with one hand?"

I rushed to answer the second question so that I could avoid the first.

"Of course!" I said. "You are young and handsome and rich and once you have recovered from your wound, you will be healthy. You will come back a hero of the great Battle of Lepanto! There will be lots of ladies ready to fall in love with you!"

I believed it. But I couldn't imagine what would happen to me. I felt more and more aware of the difference between his family and mine.

Even the most grateful noble wouldn't want his sister to marry a carpenter's son.

15

My Angel

We were all desperate for some fresh food by the time we got back to Corfu. The fleet rested there, while carpenters repaired the ships and the men got something decent to eat.

But at last we had to take to the sea again.

I was very different from the seasick boy who had travelled down from Venice in August. Then I had thought it would be glamorous to fight in a battle. I knew better now.

The men's spirits rose as we got nearer to home. On the first galley the crew all tied turbans round their heads and danced on the decks. The people of Venice would think that the Ottomans had won and were bringing back a captured fleet!

But it wasn't long before we could see all the crowds gathered in the Piazzetta and they realised the joke. A great shout went up from the crowd and I felt proud. We had won and some of us at least had come back home.

Not Nico.

It took ages for each galley to land at the Piazzetta. Then each man went ashore with his bundle and his treasure and a small crew took the ship back to the Arsenale.

I could hear shrieks as women spotted their husbands, and parents their sons. And then sobbing as other people were told of their losses. But the main sound was of cheering and joy.

At last it was *The Angel*'s turn.

Daniele insisted that we should walk down the gangplank together. I was carrying his bags to help him out – I had little enough of my own.

We could see our Captain, Giovanni Angelo, kissing a woman who must have been his wife. I wondered how, in all these crowds, anyone could spot a loved one. The crowds seemed to get bigger by the minute.

The Captain stayed near the ship and waited for us.

Then I saw Angelina. She was with a woman who must have been her mother, and an older man – her father, I was sure. The women cried out when they saw Daniele and I felt him tense beside me.

I put down his bags and was trying to slip away, but Daniele put his good arm round me and pulled me into the group. Captain Angelo was also looking at me and talking to the Santo family.

"This boy," he said, "is the reason your son is alive. Yes, Daniele has lost his hand and you may weep for that, ladies. But without young Luca's brave act, he would have lost his life."

Angelina saw me for the first time. "Luca?" she said. "Is this true?"

"Yes," her brother said. "I owe him my life and while that is beyond price, I can give him this reward."

He took out a heavy bag of coins from his coat and gave it to me. And then the Captain gave me another to match!

There was excited clapping in the crowd and, before I knew what was happening, people were carrying me on their shoulders into the Piazza San Marco.

The biggest ever party was going on there. The wine was flowing and there were stalls full of the most delicious dishes in Venice to eat. I didn't have to pay for anything. Everyone treated me as a hero.

It was nice in a way, but I was looking around all the people, trying to see my family. Angelina had disappeared long ago – gone with her parents and Daniele back to their grand house.

And then my family were all around me. My mother and father, my big sisters and brothers – hugging and kissing me.

No one told me off for running away, and soon they had heard the rumours going through the crowd that I had done something heroic.

All of a sudden I felt very tired.

"There you are!" a familiar voice said, and I found myself in a hug so tight I could hardly breathe.

It was my dear friend Fina!

She seemed to be crying. "You came back!" she said. "You are alive! I thought I'd never see you again."

It was as if the sun had come out from behind a big black cloud. I realised that I had been a fool. It was Fina I had been missing, Fina I was so very pleased to see again. Angelina was a lovely dream, but Fina was the girl I really knew and who knew me.

I hugged her right back. And then I kissed her. I gave her my rosary, the one we had all been given when we set out. It was the only pretty thing I owned.

I held on tight to Fina's hand. I didn't know what the future would be but I felt sure she would be in it. I had found my Angel of Venice.

*

I didn't know until our wedding day that Fina was short for Serafina. She told me that it meant a higher kind of angel. So I was right!

With the money from the Captain and Daniele, and more that came from the city, I was able to buy us a nice little house. It had a small garden with fruit trees. I was a master carpenter by then, but I wanted to be sure we always had enough peaches and apricots.

I stayed on friendly terms with Daniele and Angelina, even making furniture for them when they each married members of the nobility of Venice.

But the best piece I ever crafted was a jointed, polished hand for Daniele. It was so admired that people came to my workshop from all over Venice so that I could make them new limbs in place of those they had lost.

Because Lepanto was not the last battle, even though it was the last one I was ever in. And the last one I ever want to be in.

I am a man of peace now.

And I live in Venice with my angel.

Sea-faring Terms in Angel *of* Venice

Shipyard

A place where ships are built.

Forge

A blacksmith's workshop with a furnace to melt metal.

Prow

The pointed part of the front of a ship.

Stern

The back part of a ship.

Galley

A low, flat ship with one or more sails and oars. Galleys were used in war and also by merchants and pirates.

Galleass

A large, heavy galley with more rowers, sails and guns.

Pilot

An expert sailor who guides ships across difficult or busy stretches of water, often into port.

Quartermaster

The officer on the galley who looks after food, clothing and other supplies.

Bosun

The sailor in charge of the deck crew.

Our books are tested
for children and young people by
children and young people.

Thanks to everyone who consulted on
a manuscript for their time and effort in
helping us to make our books better
for our readers.